Hooey Higgins and the Big Day Out

For Tory x
S.V.

For Jen Jago, with love and thanks
E.D.

HOOEY HIGGINS
and the
Big
Day Out

STEVE VOAKE

illustrated by Emma Dodson

WALKER
BOOKS

First published 2012 by Walker Books Ltd
87 Vauxhall Walk, London SE11 5HJ

2 4 6 8 10 9 7 5 3 1

Text © 2012 Steve Voake
Illustrations © 2012 Emma Dodson

The right of Steve Voake and Emma Dodson to be identified as author and illustrator respectively of this work has been asserted by them in accordance with the Copyright, Designs and Patents Act 1988

This book has been typeset in StempelSchneidler and EDodson

Printed and bound in Great Britain
by Clays Ltd, St Ives plc

British Library Cataloguing in Publication Data:
a catalogue record for this book is available from the British Library

ISBN 978-1-4063-3429-6

www.walker.co.uk

CONTENTS

PANTS AND PANDAS

"How long are we going for again?" asked Twig as Miss Troutson closed the piano and picked up her copy of *TV Quick*.

"Just for the day," said Hooey. "We're coming back tonight, remember?"

"That's a relief," said Twig. "I was worried I hadn't packed enough pants."

"How many *have* you packed?"

"Thirteen."

"Why?"

"It's my lucky number. Plus I watched Alan Titchmarsh last night and he said you can never have enough pants."

"Plants, Twig. He was talking about plants."

"Ah well. Same difference."

Hooey was about to ask how it could possibly be the same difference when Mr Croft the headteacher stood up and began to speak in his Assembly voice.

Now remember, everyone, you will need to be on your best behaviour.

You are not going to a holiday camp. You are going to an outdoor education centre in Wales, where you will learn to step outside of your comfort zones. Isn't that right, Miss Troutson?"

"Yeah, right, absolutely," said Miss Troutson, thumbing through an article on 'Secret Lives of the Stars'. "Couldn't agree more."

Twig put up his hand. "Will you be stepping outside of your comfort zone, Miss Troutson?" he asked.

"Trust me, child," replied Miss Troutson, rolling up the magazine and putting it in her bag. "I've been outside it for years."

* * *

"Did you see *The Wizard of Oz* on Sky last night?" Twig asked Hooey as they walked towards the coach. "There's this girl called Dorothy who sings and dances along a Yellow Brick Road and then helps people find the things they need."

"What kind of things?"

"A brain, a heart and some courage," said Twig. "That's what I'm going to do on this trip."

"What, dance around in a dress?"

"I think he means he's going to help people find some new and special qualities," said Sarah-Jane Silverton.

Twig nodded. "Although I like the sound of the dancing bit."

Hooey looked at him. "Glad I brought my camera."

* * *

13

Twig reached for his bag and loosened the zip to let his toy panda breathe. Wayne Burkett pointed at him and grinned.

"What's up?" he asked. "Scared your ickle teddy bear's going to choke?"

"For your information, Mr Frobisher is *not* a teddy bear," said Twig. "He's a panda. And pandas don't like small spaces."

Don't put him in your brain then!

sniggered Wayne.

"Why have you brought him anyway?" asked Hooey.

"Next door's dog chewed up my Peppa Pig this morning," said Twig. "When I saw the way he was looking at Mr Frobisher I knew I had to bring him with me."

"Maybe you can do your Dorothy thing and help him find a brain," suggested Hooey.

Twig watched Samantha Curbitt talking to the coach driver and whispered, "*Or maybe I could help someone find a heart.*"

Hooey stared at the tattoos on the coach driver's arms.

"You could try," he said, "but I don't think he'd thank you for it."

All right, everyone!

called Miss Troutson, waving her clipboard. "I want to see your bottoms on that bus, *pronto*!"

"She's not seeing mine," said Twig. "Fact."

Miss Troutson gave him such a withering look that he jumped back and clonked his head on the coach mirror.

Ba-doing!

said Wayne. **"Smack on the coconut."**

"Oi!" shouted the bus driver as Twig clutched his head.

"I only just cleaned that."

"Sorry," said Twig, giving the mirror a squeaky wipe with his hand. "Better?"

"**Yeah**," said the bus driver, holding up a hairy fist.

Better watch out!

"Have you told him you get coach-sick?" asked Hooey as they climbed the bus steps.

"It never came up," said Twig. "Get it?"

Outside, Hooey's brother, Will, stood glumly in line, waiting to get on. "Will's worried because he hasn't invented anything for a while," explained Hooey. "He thinks he might have forgotten how to do it."

"I'm like that with toast," said Twig. "Although luckily my nan's written down the instructions."

"Outstanding," said Hooey.

"I thought Will was working on that new alarm clock for your grandpa. The one that shouted 'Fire!' and turned on his electric blanket."

"Bit of a setback there," said Hooey. "He overloaded the plug and set fire to Grandpa's duvet. Certainly woke him up though."

Twig nodded, then took out a card and started writing on it.

"What you doing?" asked Hooey.

"Mum wants me to send her a postcard. I thought I'd do it before things got too busy."

"But you've written 'Wish you were here' on it."

"So?"

"So it's a postcard of Shrimpton-on-Sea, Twig. She already *is* here."

Twig shrugged. "She likes it here."

As the bus pulled away, Hooey thought about what Mr Croft had said about stepping outside their comfort zones.

He imagined a large gorilla stomping into the lounge, pulling him off the sofa and throwing him through the window. He wondered if it was something like that and decided he didn't fancy it much.

"All right, Hooey?" asked Will, poking his head through the seats.

"Need anything inventing?"

"Not really," said Hooey. "I was just wondering if there were any gorillas in Wales."

"Only Basbo," sniggered Twig.

At the mention of his name, Basbo – who was sitting three rows down next to Ricky Mears – turned and glared at Twig. His eyebrows seemed even closer together than normal and he ground his teeth as if he had a mouthful of gravel.

"What chew frampin' off about y'lil weenburger?"

he grunted.

Come overeer unnsayitt un I'll wop ya in the wooberries!

"I didn't say anything," squeaked Twig. "Tell him, Hooey."

Hooey thought quickly. "He was talking about yoghurts," he said.

"Yum-yarts?" grunted Basbo.

"That's the ones," said Hooey. "I asked Twig if he thought there were any vanillas in Wales, and he said, 'Only Rasbo.' By which I'm thinking he meant raspberry, as in raspberry-flavoured ones."

"Yum-yarts?" said Basbo again.

"Whatever," said Twig. "Just don't kill me."

Basbo pointed a finger at him.

"Keeloooh," he said. Then he went back to his pickled-onion-flavoured Monster Munch.

"Great," said Twig gloomily. "I'm already out of my comfort zone and we're only five minutes up the road." He opened his lunchbox. "Maybe a bit of healthy eating will cheer me up. Part of my five-a-day."

"Twig, it's only quarter to nine," said Hooey as Twig unwrapped a chocolate bar.

"Well you know what they say," said Twig. "Quarter to nine, Twixy-Twix Time. And anyway, chocolate's good for your digestion." He finished off the Twix and took out a Sherbet Fountain, which left a packet of cheese and onion crisps, a Mars bar, two Crunchies and a small box of chocolate raisins.

23

"I think I already know the answer to this," said Hooey, "but did you pack your own lunchbox?"

"Certainly did," said Twig, shaking the packet of raisins. "With some extra fruity fibre for a balanced diet."

From the other side of the aisle, Sarah-Jane Silverton watched him tip sherbet into his mouth.

That's disgusting,

she said.

"If you don't like your face," said Twig, "then don't look in the window." He sniggered, breathed in at the wrong moment and snorted half a tube of sherbet up his nose.

"Ah-PHOO!" he sneezed, banging his head against the window.

Ah-PHOO!

Ahhhhh-PHOO!

Hooey held his hand out across the aisle, like a surgeon about to perform an operation.

"**Tissue**," he said.

"**Tissue**," repeated Sarah-Jane, pressing a tissue into his outstretched palm.

Hooey handed it to Twig and as Twig wiped his nose, he held his hand out again.

"**Notebook**," he said.

"**Notebook**," repeated Sarah-Jane, handing him her notebook.

Hooey turned to Twig, looked at him sadly and then cracked him over the head with it.

"Ow!" said Twig. "What was that for?"

"For eating your lunch at nine in the morning," said Hooey. "If you carry on like that you're going to be sick."

"Who are you, my mum?"

"No, I'm the person sitting next to you."

At that moment the bus swerved, sending several children tumbling into the aisle.

Yurg! shouted Basbo, climbing off the flattened figure of Johnny Bertram.

Wassa driveyman doin' wivva wivvlywob steerywheel?

"Calm *down*, Barry," said Miss Troutson. "And the rest of you, get back in your seats immediately!"

As Johnny Bertram staggered back to his seat, Hooey turned to Twig and pointed out of the window.

"Look, Twig, we're going to the service station. You know what that means, don't you?"

"What?"

"More sweets!" Hooey looked at Twig and noticed that he had turned an interesting shade of green. "Uh-oh," he said. "Will, can you invent an anti-sick device?"

"I'd take everything out of his lunchbox," said Will.

"Why?" asked Hooey, removing the rest of Twig's sweets. "Are you going to invent something now?"

Twig grabbed his lunchbox, leaned over it and made a

bleaaaargh

sound.

"Oh," said Hooey. "I see."

DANCING DISASTER

"The coach driver has kindly agreed to stop at the service station so you can visit the toilets," said Miss Troutson as everyone began to scramble into the aisle. "After all, we don't want any accidents."

Bit late for that,

said Twig.

As they left the coach, Hooey noticed Twig's panda, Mr Frobisher, hanging out of his bag.

"He's never been to a service station before," Twig explained. "I thought it was time to take him out of his comfort zone."

"Now then," said Miss Troutson as

they gathered together outside Burger King, "you've got ten minutes to go to the toilet and stretch your legs."

"Bit of a weird thing to do in the toilet," said Twig.

"I think she means afterwards," said Hooey.

"Or maybe she's talking about *dancing*," said Twig. He pointed towards the games arcade, where there was a Dance Machine with lots of flashing  lights on the floor. "Look! Samantha's going on it. Quick, give me a pound."

"Why?"

"Because I need it."

"So do I," said Hooey. "Crunchies don't buy themselves, you know."

"I'll pay you back."

Hooey sighed, fished in his pocket and handed Twig a pound coin. "All right. But this had better be worth it. I could've bought two Crunchies with that."

Will patted him on the shoulder. "A Crunchie is a wonderful thing, Hooey," he said, "but like a beautiful sunset, the memory soon fades. Whereas the sight of Twig making a fool of himself is something that will last for ever."

"You pay for him then," said Hooey.

Can't, said Will. "I spent all my money on Crunchies."

Twig stood next to Samantha, clutching his pound coin. "The lights can be our Yellow Brick Road, Samantha," he said happily. "Let's dance down it and find you a heart!"

"Now you're just being weird," said Samantha.

"That's what they said to Lady Gaga." said Twig.

He pushed his money into the slot and the music started. As the signs flashed and the bass thumped across the arcade, they both began to dance. At first they moved slowly, watching the colours on the screen and stepping on the lights beneath their feet in time with the music. But then the lights started flashing more quickly and soon Twig and Samantha were jumping, twisting and swapping places with each other as the music got faster and everyone crowded around to watch.

"Wow," said Will. "Twig's actually pretty good."

"Come on, Samantha!" Twig yelled,
leaping from green light to yellow. "Let's go
down the Road together!"

He spun around with a "**Wooh!**"

and a

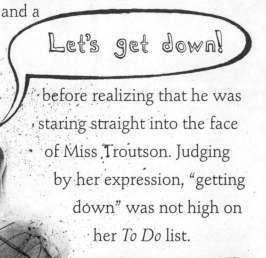

Let's get down!

before realizing that he was
staring straight into the face
of Miss Troutson. Judging
by her expression, "getting
down" was not high on
her *To Do* list.

Twig screamed, staggered backwards and flipped over the safety bar before landing directly on the head of Basbo, who had just that second purchased a Mr Whippy ice cream with chocolate sauce and two chocolate flakes. As Twig flumped down onto his head, Basbo's hand flew up and smacked the ice cream into his face. Both of them skidded sideways and smashed into the front of the Fairground Penny Pusher.

"**Oi!**" shouted the man from the change booth, rapping on his window as a tide of copper pennies poured out onto Basbo's head.

Wha chew fink you're playin' at?

Slowly, Basbo
touched his cheek
and stared at the
chocolate sauce on
the end of his finger.

"*I think,*" whispered Twig, noticing that Basbo had ice cream all over his face and a flake up each nostril, "*you might have missed a bit.*"

BRICK ROADS
AND BISCUITS

When they arrived at the activity centre,
everyone sat on the grass while the centre
manager, Mr Evans, introduced himself.

"What are we all here to have?"
he asked.

Twig put his hand up.
"Biscuits?"

"**No**," replied Mr Evans sternly. "**That is not the answer I was looking for.**"

Hooey could tell from the way Mr Evans' chin jutted out that he wasn't someone who wasted time on biscuits when there were rivers to cross or mountains to climb.

I'll ask again,

he said, cupping a hairy hand to his ear. "**What are we here to have?**"

Fun!

shouted everyone,
although Ricky Mears
shouted it so loud that his
voice went all high and he
had to hold on to his eyes
in case they popped out.

"That is correct," said Mr Evans.
"But with great fun comes
great responsibility."

He turned to Hooey. "Tell me, son, have you ever been up to your neck in a crocodile-infested swamp with enemy soldiers tracking your every move?" Hooey thought for a moment.

I don't think so.

"Of *course* you haven't," said Mr Evans, "and neither have I. But if I had, I'd be saying exactly the same to you as I'm going to say now. And you know what that is?"

"Bring plenty of biscuits," said Twig.

Mr Evans frowned. "What is it with you and biscuits?"

"You can use them to distract the crocodiles," said Twig. "They've been chewing on dead antelopes for the past gazillion years. So you give 'em a whiff of a Chocolate Hobnob and they go mad for it. And when they do, you can leg it off into the jungle."

Hooey nodded. "He's right, y'know."

Mr Evans stared at them as if they were from a different planet. Then he looked around the rest of the group.

"The answer I'm looking for," he said, "is: Leave your comfort zones behind and be ready for new opportunities."

Ooh! .said Twig, putting his hand up. "Also, we can help people find their courage and their brains and their *hearts*." He looked at Samantha and gave her a little wave.

"Very good!"

said Mr Evans, smiling broadly. "Now you're getting the idea!"

"Just like Dorothy in *The Wizard of Oz*!" said Twig.

The instructor stopped smiling. "I don't know about that, son," he said. "We're here to toughen up. And to do that we're going to need Discipline, Commitment and Perseverance."

Twig looked at Hooey.

"They must be the other instructors," he said.

* * *

After lunch, Will went off with the older group while Hooey and Twig were put in a group with Basbo, Samantha, Yasmin and Sarah-Jane Silverton.

Their instructor was a tanned, blond-haired Australian called Dave who looked as if he had stepped straight out of a surfing movie.

All right, mates,

he said, pulling down the cuffs of his wetsuit, "who fancies a little trip on the water?"

Sarah-Jane wanted to
know if the water had
been tested for germs
and Basbo shouted

Shark!

every time the sun went behind
a cloud, but soon they were
all pulling on wetsuits and
making their way across to
the river bank.

"Hnnnf!"

said Twig as he got his head stuck in the top of his wetsuit. "Nigh fink nive got na-nong size."

"It's not the size so much," said Hooey. "It's more to do with the fact that you've shoved your head through one of the legs."

Hooey grabbed the wetsuit, stood on Twig's feet and pulled as hard as he could.

There was a squeaking sound as the rubber
peeled away from Twig's face and then his
head popped out and the wetsuit flew across
the grass, knocking Sarah-Jane Silverton off
her feet.

Sharky-shark!

screamed Basbo.

Sharky-shark
come outta
warty an
gobbler up!

Before Hooey had a chance to explain, Basbo snatched the wetsuit off Sarah-Jane, threw it to the ground and began jumping up and down on it. "Bad sharky-shark!" he shouted.

"Sharky-shark gonna geddit inna whamsies!"

"Easy there, mate," said Dave, pulling Basbo away and patting him on the arm. "It's only a wetsuit. See?"

He held it up and Basbo stared at it for a few seconds.

"Sharky-shark ded now," he said, peering into the neck of the wetsuit. "Ollis teefallen out."

"That's it, mate," said Dave, stepping back and holding the wetsuit out to Twig behind his back. "Whatever you say."

Sarah-Jane Silverton looked at Basbo and smiled. "My knight in shining armour," she said.

"Yeah right," said Twig. "More like a night out in Nutsford."

"Well you'd know all about that," said Samantha.

Twig put his thumb up to Hooey and grinned. "Samantha thinks I'm intelligent!"

He stuffed his head
back into his wetsuit
and Hooey watched
it bulge through the
rubber.

"I think they forgot
to put a hole in this
one," said Twig in a
muffled voice.

"Either that," said
Hooey, "or you've put
it on upside down."

The outline of
Twig's face appeared
through the rubber,
looking surprised
and disappointed at
the same time.

Maybe we
won't tell anyone
about this,

he said.

* * *

"Now these little fellas are what's known as kayaks," said Dave, pointing at the row of yellow boats lined up on the river bank. "The idea is that you sit in them and use your paddles to take you where you want to go."

"My auntie used to take me where I wanted to go," said Twig. "She sat me in the sidecar of her motorbike and took me to Bingo. Sometimes they let me call out the numbers."

"What, like: Six and four: sixty-four?" asked Hooey.

"Yeah. All the eights: twenty-seven!"

"I'm guessing they didn't let you do it very often," said Hooey.

Twig frowned.

"How did you know?"

Hooey sat in his kayak and watched Dave push Twig's boat into the river.

"I'm too young to die, Hooey!" squeaked Twig as he wobbled from side to side. "But if I do, you can have my trainers."

"Lucky me," said Hooey.

"ALL RIGHT, EVERYONE," Dave called, "we're going to raft up! Paddle over here next to my old mate Twig, and hold on to each other's kayaks so that we're all in one long line. Got it?"

shouted everyone, except for
Twig, who kept saying, "I'm his old
mate! I'm his old mate!"

After a few bumps and spins, Hooey
eventually found himself floating between
Samantha and Basbo, who was on the very
end of the line.

"**ALL RIGHT, EVERYONE**," called
Dave, "lay your paddles in front of you,
then hold on to the boat to your left."

As Hooey grabbed on to Basbo's boat,
Basbo splashed his hand down into the
water and stared around wildly.

"Wheresa boat gone?" he grunted.
"Boaty dista-purred!" He pulled his
hand out of the water and stared at Hooey.
"Sharky come eat nimmup!"

"Don't worry," said Hooey, trying to keep
Basbo calm, "you're the last one in the line."

Basbo looked at the line
of boats to his right, then
at the water, then back
at Hooey.

*Eyesa lassunn
innna line,*

he said quietly.
"*Uh lassunn inna line.*"

"ALL RIGHT, LISTEN UP,
MATES," said Dave, paddling
his kayak around to face them.
"What we're going to do
now is the Test of Courage.
Anyone guess what
that is?"

Twig put his hand up. "Do we have to paddle around without screaming?"

"Well that would be a start," said Dave, "but in the meantime you might want to put your hand back on the other kayak."

Twig looked down, saw that he was drifting away and screamed.

shouted Basbo.

"*I think we all need to chill out a bit, mates,*" said Dave, paddling over and pushing Twig back into line. "It's no use trying to pass the Test of Courage if you're all shriekin' and sharkin' about stuff."

"*Sharky foll-slarm,*" said Basbo. "*Gotta watchem tho annyew?*"

Hooey wondered whether Basbo actually thought sharks lived in *all* kinds of water. If so, he guessed bath time was probably a bit of a problem in the Basbo household. And as for going to the toilet...

"*So here's what you do,*" said Dave, standing up in his kayak and holding out his arms. "When it's your turn, you have to get up

66

and then the rest of us slap our kayaks and shout 'GO, GO, GO!' Like that. Let's have a try. Ready? And…"

"Go, go, go!" shouted everyone, drumming on the sides of their kayaks. "Go, go, go, go, go!"

"Very good," said Dave, "but that's not all of it."

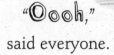

"Oooh," said everyone.

"Oooh is right," said Dave. "Because what happens next is, you have to walk across the front of all the other kayaks until you get to the end. Then you have to do a little victory dance and walk all the way back and sit down again."

There was a buzz of excitement followed by lots of squealing and nervous laughter.

"So who wants to go first?" Dave asked when the noise had died down. "Who's feeling brave enough to take the Test of Courage?"

"Me," said Samantha. "I'll do it." Hooey heard a gasp of admiration and saw that Twig was gazing at her from the other end of the line.

DON'T WORRY, SAMANTHA!

he called, pointing along the row of boats. "Just think of it as our very own Yellow Brick Road!"

"Save it, Numpty," said Samantha.

"Spoken like a true lady," said Dave. "Ready?"

Samantha stood up, stepped daintily onto the front of her kayak and nodded.

"Ready."

"Go!" shouted everyone, drumming their hands against the sides of the boats. "Go, go, go, go, go!"

69

Samantha walked coolly across the kayaks
as if she was simply going for a stroll in the
park. When she got to Twig's kayak she did
a little Hawaiian dance, skipped back
along the line and sat
down again.

HULA-HULA!

shouted Twig, standing up as
everyone clapped and cheered.
"My turn now! Time to find
my courage, eh, Samantha?"
    "What's he talking about?"
asked Samantha.

"That film *The Wizard of Oz*," explained Hooey. "That's why he keeps going on about Yellow Brick Roads."

"Maybe he should try looking for his brain first," said Yasmin. "And while he's doing that, I'm going next!"

She stood up, wobbled her way to the end of the boats and then ran back again in double-quick time.

"Nice work," said Dave, turning to look at Hooey.

"Your turn next, mate. Time to find *your* courage!"

Hooey secretly thought he would be much happier finding a TV and a packet of Chocolate Hobnobs. But he guessed that wasn't an option.

"Go!" shouted everyone, slapping their hands on the sides of the boats. "Go, go, go, go, go!"

Holding his arms out to steady himself, Hooey carefully put one foot on the front of Samantha's boat. It felt like stepping onto a soft mattress and for a moment he thought he was going to lose his balance. But, keeping his arms out like a tightrope-walker, he finally made it all the way to Twig's boat.

"YES!" Hooey shouted. "SHOW ME TO THE WIZARD!"

Then he turned, tripped and fell face first into the river.

"It's not so bad once you're in," said
Hooey, swimming back to his kayak. "Cools
you down nicely."

"Your turn, Twig," he called, pulling a
piece of duck weed from his mouth. "Just
think of it as your Yellow Brick Road!"

Twig grinned. "I'm going to find courage!"
he shouted. "I'm going to find a brain! And
then I'm going to find a heart for Samantha!"

He ran along the row of boats, screamed
and fell off the end of Basbo's kayak.

"**Bleeg!**" cried Basbo as Twig disappeared into the river. "**Eeez lookin' fur sharkies!**" Then he stood up and threw himself over the side.

"**Creeping kangaroos!**" said Dave. "Now there's two of 'em in the drink."

As Dave dived in, Hooey looked down at his own dripping wetsuit, shrugged and jumped in too.

Twig swam up to the surface, popped his head out of the water and looked at Hooey. "Are you the Wizard of Oz?" he wheezed.

"No," said Hooey. "Are you the Scarecrow without a brain?"

"Actually, I'm not," said Twig. "I'm the Tin Man."

He lifted his hand out of the water and Hooey saw that he was holding a can of beer.

"Found it on the bottom," said Twig. "I wonder if there's any more down there?"

"Never mind that," said Hooey, "I think Dave needs a hand."

Dave was trying to rescue Basbo, but every time he grabbed him Basbo jumped into the air shouting,

"Sharky-shark, sharky-shark, sharky-shark!"

Finally, Basbo pulled something from the water, threw it onto the bank and shouted,

Sharky-shark, NO!

Then he swam back to his boat, climbed in and sat with his arms folded, staring into space.

On the bank,
a man in a black wetsuit
was lying on the grass, holding his head.

"Alwyn, are you all right?" asked Dave, wading out of the water.

"*It's Mr Evans,*" whispered Twig as they climbed back into their boats. "*He looks a bit shocked.*"

"I'm not surprised," said Hooey. "It can't be every day he gets mistaken for a shark."

"That kid's a genius," said Mr Evans, shaking his head.

"*Does he mean Basbo?*" whispered Twig.

"*I think he does,*" said Hooey.

"I thought I had all my bases covered, but he came out of nowhere, Dave. He came out of nowhere."

"What were you doing in the river?" asked Dave. "I thought you had the afternoon off."

"A good Marine never has time off," said Mr Evans. "A good Marine swims out to check on his staff unnoticed. But that kid ... that kid's a professional." He stood up and walked to the edge of the river bank.

HEY, KID!

he shouted at Basbo.
"Were you ever in the Marines?"

Basbo stared at him and shook his head. "No talk to sharky-sharks," he said. "Sharky-sharks bad."

Hooey turned to Twig. "Glad you helped Basbo find his brain," he said. "How's it going with the courage and the heart bit?"

"Well I screamed when I fell off the kayak," said Twig, "and Samantha just called me a loser. But apart from that, everything's fine."

As they took off their wetsuits and made their way back to the centre, Hooey decided to try and cheer Twig up.

"We've got another exercise later," he told him, "so that means you've still got time to find the Oz things before we go home. Let's get changed and see how Mr Frobisher's getting on."

MR FROBISHER!

cried Twig happily.

"I nearly forgot!"

He ran to his locker,
pulled out his bag,
unzipped it and began
frantically rummaging around.
"What is it?" asked
Hooey. "What's the matter?"

Twig dropped his bag, sat down
and put his head in his hands.

"It's Mr Frobisher," he whispered.
"He's gone."

HOOEY FLIES HIGH

"You should eat something," said Hooey, patting Twig's arm and offering him a peanut-butter sandwich. "Keep your strength up."

"I can't eat at a time like this," said Twig, taking the sandwich and eating it. "I can't believe I've lost Mr Frobisher. I brought him with me to keep him safe and look what's happened."

"But you took him out of his comfort zone," said Hooey, "and that's got to be a good thing. Mr Croft said so."

"Yeah, but he also said that Santa was coming to the school fair last year and it turned out to be Mrs Gumbleton with a beard."

"She gave us two free Crunchies though," said Hooey. "Look, maybe you left him on the coach. We can check later when we get back on."

Twig stuck out his lower lip. "He'd have been better off with next door's dog. Did you see the driver's face when he heard I'd been sick on his coach?"

"Not a pretty sight," agreed Hooey. "Mind you, neither was your lunchbox."

Before Twig could say anything more, Mr Evans raised one arm in the air and shouted:

MARINES, FALL IN!

Hooey and Twig looked over at Miss Troutson, who was sitting contentedly in a deckchair. She held a half-eaten Snickers bar in one hand and a holiday brochure in the other.

"If that's being out of your comfort zone," said Hooey, "then throw me through the window."

Miss Troutson saw them staring and waved them away with the back of her hand.

"Off you go, boys," she said. "I'd love to join you, but I get vertigo."

"What's vertigo?" asked Twig as they followed Mr Evans down a narrow lane through a wood.

"Probably a magazine," said Hooey, "about sitting in deckchairs eating chocolate."

"Sounds good to me," said Twig. "I wonder where you order it from?"

"Vertigo isn't a magazine," said Sarah-Jane, who had been listening to their conversation. "Vertigo means you're afraid of heights."

"What's that got to do with anything?" asked Twig. "We're not exactly going to be spending the afternoon up Mount Everest."

At the end of the lane, Mr Evans opened
a gate and they walked out of the trees
into a field. Around the outside of the
field was a fence. And in the middle of
the field was a collection of the thickest,
tallest poles that Hooey had ever seen.
All of them were connected with ladders,
nets and pieces of rope. In front of them
was a big sign which said:

DANGER
HIGH ROPES COURSE

"Ulp," said Hooey.

"Neat," said Samantha.

"I think I've got vertigo," said Twig. "Can I go and lie down?"

"It's very simple," said Mr Evans. "All you have to do is climb this pole, stand on the platform at the top and wave to your friends. Then you scramble across the net to the platform on the other side, where Jenny will show you what to do next."

Hooey looked at the
ladder propped against
the tall pole in front of
them. He stared at the tiny
wooden platform at the
top and then at the other
one in the distance where
a lady instructor was
waving at them.

"Is that Jenny over there?" asked Twig nervously.

"That's her, son," said Mr Evans. "And when you get there you have to give her the secret password which allows you to complete the course."

"What *is* the secret password?" asked Yasmin.

Mr Evans smiled and pointed up at a small white square taped beneath the platform above them. "See that? All you have to do is look underneath and rearrange the letters to find it."

Peecy paper

said Basbo.
"Peecy peecy
paper!"

And before Mr Evans
could stop him, he ran forward
and began climbing the ladder.

"That's m'boy!" said Mr Evans,
grabbing the back of Basbo's
shorts. "Fearless, he is. But we'd
better do it properly, just in case."

He clipped a safety rope onto Basbo's harness and then let go of his shorts. Basbo grasped the ladder, grunted, then shot up the pole like a monkey who had just remembered where he'd left his bananas.

"Now remember, we're all here to learn lessons," said Mr Evans. "That boy up there jumped on me in the river and it taught me always to be on my guard. The important thing is, once you've learned a lesson, you should never make the same mistake again."

He looked up and down, this way and that.

See? ALWAYS on my guard.

"And always off his rocker," whispered Hooey.

"I heard that, son," said Mr Evans. "OK, get roped up. You're next."

Hooey swallowed nervously and pulled on his harness. As he watched Basbo leaning over the edge of the platform, his stomach flipped and for the first time in his life he wished he was sitting in a deckchair next to Miss Troutson.

"Nuf!"

shouted Basbo from the top
of the platform.

"GET A GRIP, SON,"
Mr Evans shouted back. "A good Marine
never has enough. A good Marine
just keeps on going. So show 'em
what you can do, boy!"

"Nuf!" shouted Basbo.
"Nuf! Nuf!
Nuf!"

Then
he spread
his arms,
belly-flopped
onto the
netting and
scuttled off like a
spring-loaded spider.

When he reached
the far side, he climbed
onto the platform and shouted,
"Nuf!" once more. Jenny attached
his harness to a zip-wire and, with a
blood-curdling scream, he leapt off the
platform, whizzed down the wire and
disappeared into the trees.

"Well they won't need to bury him,
that's for sure," said Twig. "By the time
they find what's left of him he'll be
halfway to Australia."

"OK, soldier," said
Mr Evans, tapping
Hooey on the
shoulder.
"Your turn."

It wasn't too bad at first. Hooey could hear people's voices fading as he climbed higher and higher. It was actually quite peaceful with the sound of the birds and the whisper of the breeze. But then he made the mistake of looking down and when he saw how high up he was and how small everyone appeared, his legs turned to jelly. He quickly reminded himself of what Mr Croft had said about comfort zones.

Then, taking a deep
breath, he reached up
for the next rung of
the ladder. When he
finally got to the top,
he pulled himself up
onto the platform and
sat clutching the edge,
trying not to look down.

THAT'S IT!

shouted Mr Evans from
down below. "NOW
LOOK FOR THE
PASSWORD!"

Gripping the edges of the platform, Hooey leaned over and peered underneath. At first he couldn't see anything, but then he spotted a piece of paper with three letters written on it. The letters were:

It was a few moments before he realized that if he rearranged the letters, they spelled out FUN. And it was a few more moments before he realized that Basbo had simply been reading the letters as they were written and thought the password was "NUF".

With his hands trembling and heart pounding, Hooey stood up and took a deep breath. Then he jumped off the platform and launched himself into space. As he landed on the netting he realized a) that he hadn't been killed and b) that Mr Croft was actually right about moving out of your comfort zone. It might be a bit scary, but once you had done it, it was something else too.

It was **FUN**!

Hooey scrambled across the net and pulled himself up onto the platform on the other side. He smiled as he heard a cheer go up behind him and then Jenny the instructor unclipped his safety harness and attached it to the zip-wire.

"Do you know the password?" she asked.

"It's **FUN**," said Hooey. "Fun, fun, fun, fun, fun!"

Jenny winked at him. "If you think that was fun, just wait until you've had a go on this."

She led Hooey to the edge of the platform and pointed towards the trees. "Are you ready to fly?" she asked.

The butterflies that had been fluttering in Hooey's stomach suddenly decided to invite all their friends around for a party.

"I'm ready," he said.

Then he stepped off the platform.

With a *zzzzing* sound, the world blurred at the edges and Hooey shot towards the trees at a speed which made him think about rockets and space travel. But just as he thought his head was about to come off, he zipped through the branches and landed as lightly as a kitten on a little fluffy cushion.

"OH YES," shouted Hooey, punching the air and unclipping his harness. "Just wait till I tell Twig about this!"

But by the time he got back to the others Twig was already high above them, climbing onto the platform.

"YOO-HOO, SAMANTHA," he called. "I'm off for a walk along the Yellow Brick Road!"

"You see?" said Mr Evans, when he saw Hooey. "All you need is confidence. Confidence and constant awareness."

"Mr Evans," said Hooey, who had noticed Twig wobbling around on the edge of the platform, "I think—"

"Awareness," continued Mr Evans, "is the ability to always be on your guard."

"But—"

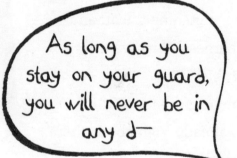

As long as you stay on your guard, you will never be in any d—

Before Mr Evans could say the word "danger", Twig fell off the platform, swung down on the safety rope and cracked him in the back of the head.

"Sorry, I didn't quite catch that," said Hooey as Mr Evans flumped down at his feet. "What was it you were saying?"

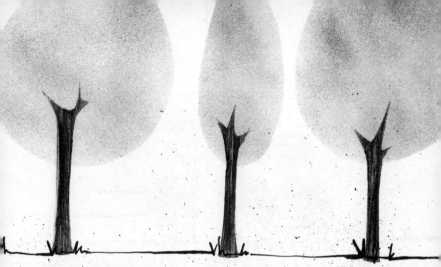

SICKATRON
SURPRISE

"I think maybe Mr Evans needs to work on his awareness," said Twig as they made their way back to the coach.

"Maybe he does," said Hooey. "Although it's not often you get cracked in the head by someone singing songs from *The Wizard of Oz*."

As they climbed the
steps of the coach, Hooey
noticed Twig was looking rather pale.

"Maybe you'd better not eat any more chocolate," he said.

"Shouldn't be a problem," said Twig, "seeing as how I've eaten it all already."

He sat down with a loud sigh and stared out of the window.

"Don't upset yourself, Twig," said Hooey. "I've still got some Pineapple Chunks if you want some."

114

"It's not that," replied Twig sadly. "It's just that I haven't done any of the things I set out to do, have I? Instead of helping people find a brain, or a heart, or some courage, all I found was a can of beer."

"Well don't let Troutson see it," said Hooey. "I don't think she likes kids drinking beer on school trips."

"Where does she like them drinking it then?"

"I don't think she likes them drinking it anywhere, Twig."

Twig sighed again. "Well that's just great. I've lost Mr Frobisher, messed up my mission and now I'm going to get it in the neck from Miss Troutson."

"But on the plus side," said Hooey, "you have eaten about four hundred tons of chocolate."

"You know what?" said Twig, pulling the can out of his bag. "I'm going to give this beer away. At least then I won't get blamed for it."

"I don't think Troutson drinks beer," said Hooey. "I think she likes Chardonnay."

"What, that girl in Year Three?"

"No, the drink, Twig."

"I'm not giving it to Troutson anyway," said Twig. "I'm giving it to the coach driver."

Hooey watched the driver crack his knuckles and stare out of the window. "Are you sure that's wise?" he asked.

But Twig was already out of his seat. He tapped the coach driver on the shoulder, shoved the can of beer in his face and shouted,

Sur-prise!

"What's this for?" growled the coach driver. "Are you having a laugh or summink?"

"No, it's a present," said Twig. "I thought you might like it."

The coach driver stared at the beer can, then back at Twig, his face softening like a toffee in summer.

"A present?" he asked. "For me?"

"Sure, why not?" said Twig. "I found it after I lost Mr Frobisher."

The coach driver frowned. "Who's Mr Frobisher?"

"He's a panda," explained Hooey, who had followed Twig to the front. Then he put his hand up to his mouth and whispered, *"He's Twig's teddy."*

For a moment the coach driver looked as if he was about to cry.

"I lost *my* teddy when I was your age," he said. "But my dad told me I should grow up and get over it."

Twig patted him on the shoulder. "What did he know?" he said.

The coach driver placed the can of beer delicately on the dashboard, as if it were a precious vase made of china.

"You and your friend sit up front here," he said to Twig, pointing to the seats behind his own. "Any time you feel sick, just let old Bob know, OK? I'll pull over until you feel right again."

"Wow," said Twig. "Thanks, Bob."

"No problem at all," said Bob. "Nothing's too much trouble for my little pal."

Twig turned to Hooey. "I'm Bob's little pal," he said.

"You won't be much longer if you do to him what you did to your lunchbox," said Hooey as the coach pulled away. "How are you feeling anyway?"

Icky, said Twig.

Will stuck his head through the seats.

"I think I might be able to help," he said. "After you were ill·this morning I invented the Will Higgins Sickatron." He pushed his lunchbox through the gap.

"Strap this on his head, Hooey."

As Hooey fastened Will's lunchbox to Twig's face with elastic bands, Will began rummaging around in his bag.

"Hang on," he said. "I've just remembered an extra-specially soothing picture."

Hooey took the box from Twig's face again and watched Will stick in a picture he'd cut from a magazine. There were already photographs of mountain streams

and peaceful woodland glades
stuck into the lunchbox,
but this one was a
white sun-kissed
beach complete with
palm trees and a
beautiful blue ocean.

"*Is it Shrimpton-on-Sea?*" whispered Twig.

"No, it's the Bahamas," said Will. "Try
making the sound of the waves, Hooey.
Create some ambience."

Hooey leaned over and made swooshing
noises in Twig's ear.

"What's that?" asked Twig, his voice
muffled by the Tupperware box.

"It's the sea," said Hooey, "splashing
against the shore."

"Sounds more like a toilet flushing," said
Twig. "Which is actually making me want
to go."

"All right, forget the sea," said Will hurriedly. "How's it looking in there?"

"It's brilliant," said Twig. "It's like I'm actually there. Except the beach smells of cheese and onion crisps."

"Which, in a way, is a bonus," said Hooey.

Twig sniffed a few times. "Also, I can smell egg mayonnaise."

"That's because Grandma put her sandwiches in there ready for her trip to Alton Towers," said Will. "But then she remembered she was going on Oblivion and decided she'd be better off leaving her lunch at home."

He tapped Twig on the shoulder. "Have you made use of all the facilities yet?"

"What facilities? All I can see is a beach."

"Look at the end of it."

Twig leaned forward in his seat, as if this would somehow help.

"Ooh, I can see something now. Is it a toy shop?"

"No, it's a beach bar," said Will. "Go ahead and order yourself a drink. It's on the house."

Twig waved his hands about as if trying to attract the attention of an imaginary barman.

"Excuse me," he said in an echoey voice,

could I have a pina colada please?

"They've only got Ribena," said Will.

"Ribena it is then," said Twig.

Will leaned over and handed Hooey some Sellotape and a juice carton.

"I've drilled a hole in the bottom of the lunchbox," he explained, "so all you have to do is stick the straw through and it'll come out over the top of the beach bar."

"Nice touch," said Hooey, sellotaping the carton to the bottom of the box. Taking the end of the straw, he twisted it round and pushed it through the hole.

"Aieee!" squeaked Twig. "Emergency, emergency! Someone just shoved a spear through the barman's head."

"Oops," said Will.

"Never mind," said Hooey. "It's not every day you get to sit on a beach drinking Ribena out of a barman's head."

As the sound of slurping echoed around the inside of the lunchbox, the coach suddenly turned off onto a slip road and came to a halt in the service station car park.

Basbo, who was sitting a few rows behind them, stared through the window at the service station and then turned to look at Twig. Deep in his mind, a memory stirred. It was something to do with Twig, an ice cream and a pair of chocolate flakes up his nose.

"I don't want to worry you, Twig," whispered Hooey, "but Basbo looks as though he might be about to kill you."

"What?" said Twig, turning round and bumping the lunchbox against the window. "Is he on the beach?"

When Miss Troutson got up to talk to the coach driver, Basbo leapt out of his seat, raised his elbow and whacked the Ribena carton on the front of the lunchbox. There was a squelching sound, a muffled squeal from Twig and then purple juice squirted out of the sides, splattering the windows, the seat covers and Sarah-Jane Silverton's sparkly new T-shirt.

I CAN'T WEAR PURPLE!

she shrieked. "It doesn't go with my eyes!"

But Basbo was already heading back down the bus and when Miss Troutson turned round to see what all the fuss was about he had knocked Ricky Mears sideways into the footwell and was sitting patiently in his seat again.

"Well done, Barry," said Miss Troutson, glaring at Sarah-Jane, who was still shrieking and trying to scrub juice off her top. "At least some of us know how to behave. Now settle down, all of you, while I find out what's going on."

Twig removed the elastic bands from his head and stared into the lunchbox, Ribena dripping off the end of his nose.

"The beach is ruined and the barman's exploded," he said.

This is the worst holiday EVER.

Hooey looked through the window and
saw that Bob the coach driver was talking to
Miss Troutson and pointing at a lorry parked
under the trees. Miss Troutson listened for
a few moments and then got back onto the
coach again.

"I have no idea why we have stopped,"
she said, "but there appears to be some
sort of problem." She glared at Hooey and
Twig. "And the coach driver thinks it's got
something to do with *you two.*"

Oh no, thought Hooey. *She's going to find
out about the beer.*

Come on, said Miss
Troutson firmly.
"We need
to get this
sorted out."

As Hooey followed Twig off the coach, he imagined Mr Croft holding up the can of beer in Assembly and pointing to them as the whole school gasped in horror. He imagined the headline in the school paper: **BOB THE BOOZY BUS DRIVER BLAMES BOYS FOR BEER.** He imagined—

"**Hooey, look**," said Twig. "Bob's calling us over."

Hooey turned and saw Bob beckoning to them from beside the lorry.

Miss Troutson sighed. "Go on then," she said. "But for heaven's sake be quick about it. *Coronation Street*'s on at seven thirty."

Twig looked at the faces pressed
against the coach window and then looked
back at Hooey.

"D'you think we're in trouble?" he asked.

"There's only one way
to find out," said Hooey.

When they reached the lorry, Bob was busy talking to the other driver.

"He gave me a can of beer," he said.

"I didn't mean to," said Twig. "I fell off a kayak."

"It was his only can, but he still gave it to me," said Bob. "And so when I heard it on the radio I thought, *No, is it? Could it be?*"

"*What's he on about?*" whispered Twig.

"*I dunno,*" whispered Hooey. "*Maybe he's drunk the beer already.*"

"D'you want to have a look then?" asked the lorry driver.

"I'm not saying it is," said Bob, turning to Hooey and Twig, "but it's worth a look, lads, isn't it? It's definitely worth a look."

Hooey could tell by the expression on Twig's face that he was as confused as Hooey was, but they followed the two men to the front of the lorry and when they got there, Bob turned and pointed to a spot just below the windscreen.

"Well?" he asked. "What d'you think?"

Twig stared at the front of the lorry and gasped. He pressed his hands to his cheeks and gave a little squeal of joy.

"That's him!" he cried. "It's him, it's him!"

And as Hooey looked up he saw that there

was a small teddy bear fixed to the front of the cab. It was a black and white one, and it was Mr Frobisher.

"But however did you find him?"

asked Twig as Bob thanked the lorry driver and handed Mr Frobisher back to his rightful owner.

"Easy," said Bob. "I remembered that lorry drivers sometimes put toys they've found on the front of their cabs. So when you told me you'd lost yours, I got on the radio and one of the drivers said he'd seen a lorry parked up here with a panda on the front. I didn't know it was yours, but I thought it was worth a try. Turns out he found it on the floor by the Dance Machine."

When they got back on the coach, a big cheer went up and even Miss Troutson had the beginnings of a smile on her face.

"I might not have done all my *Wizard of Oz* things," said Twig as the coach pulled off again, "but at least I got Mr Frobisher back."

"Hang on though," said Hooey. "You were sick on the way, right? But you weren't sick on the way back."

"So?"

"So Will saw you being sick and that made him invent the Sickatron. Which means you actually helped him find his brain."

"Wow," said Twig. He watched Samantha mouth "Numpty" at him and make an "L" shape on her forehead. "But I don't think I helped Samantha find a heart."

"Perhaps not," said Hooey, "but if you hadn't given the coach driver that can of beer, he'd never have tried to find Mr Frobisher for you. So, in a way, you helped *him* find his heart."

Twig thought for a moment. "Maybe I *am* like Dorothy," he said. Then as Basbo  turned to stare at him he added, "And maybe I shouldn't say stuff like that out loud."

"Brains, a heart *and* Mr Frobisher," said Hooey. "Not bad for a day's work."

"Shame about the courage though," said Twig. "It would've been good to get all three."

Hooey settled back in his seat and watched Bob the driver changing gear. He looked at the can of beer sitting next to him on the dashboard. Then he sat up and gave Twig a nudge.

"Twig," he said, pointing to the can of beer, "look at that."

On the bottom half of the can, printed in big letters, were the words:

BEST BITTER

And on the top half of the can, printed in even bigger letters was the word:

Twig sniggered. Hooey held out his hand for Twig to high-five. Then, as Twig's sniggers turned to wheezy giggles, they both laughed so hard that Hooey spilt Dr Pepper on his trousers and Coke  came spraying out of Twig's nose.

When Hooey finally got his breath back he asked, "So what d'you think of that then, Twig?"

Wedging his Coke can between his knees, Twig hooked his fingers in the sides of his mouth and stretched it out until he could no longer talk properly.

"As Dohwahfee fwom va *Wissard of Oss* might say," he said, staring at the end of his nose until he went cross-eyed, "I fink vat it's vewwy, vewwy ...

STEVE VOAKE (also author of the Daisy Dawson series) was born in Midsomer Norton where he spent many years falling off walls, bikes and go-karts before he got older and realized he didn't bounce like he used to. When he was Headteacher of Kilmersdon School he tried to convince children that falling off walls, bikes and go-karts wasn't such a good idea, but no one really believed him. He now enjoys writing the Hooey Higgins stories and hasn't fallen off anything for over a week.

EMMA DODSON has always been inspired by silly stories and loves drawing scruffy little animals and children. She sometimes writes and illustrates her own silly stories – including *Badly Drawn Dog* and *Speckle the Spider*. As well as drawing and painting, Emma makes disgusting things for film and TV. If you've ever seen anyone on telly get a bucket of poo thrown on them or step in a pile of sick you can be fairly sure that she was responsible for making it. Emma also teaches Illustration at the University of Westminster where she gets to talk about more sensible things.